Rusty's
RED
VACATION

by Kelly Asbury

Henry Holt and Company

New York

Henry Holt and Company, Inc.
Publishers since 1866
115 West 18th Street
New York, New York 10011

Henry Holt is a registered trademark
of Henry Holt and Company, Inc.
Copyright © 1997 by Kelly Asbury
Published in Canada by Fitzhenry & Whiteside Ltd.,
195 Allstate Parkway, Markham, Ontario L3R 4T8.

Library of Congress Cataloging-in-Publication Data
Asbury, Kelly.
Rusty's red vacation/Kelly Asbury.
Summary: On vacation, Rusty and his family
go camping in the woods.
[1. Camping—Fiction.] I. Title.
PZ7.A775Ru 1996 [E]—dc20 96-21712

ISBN 0-8050-4021-8
First Edition—1997
Typography by Martha Rago
The artist used water-soluble crayon on bristol
board to create the illustrations for this book.
Printed in the United States of America
on acid-free paper.◁▷
10 9 8 7 6 5 4 3 2 1

For my family
–K. A.

I am Rusty and this
is my dog, Ruby.
We are best friends.

Last summer,
my family took a vacation.

We stayed at a campground with lots of tall trees.

We went on hikes,

swam in a river

and went fishing.
I caught a fish!

At sundown we ate dinner cooked over the campfire.

The woods got
very dark at night.

Sometimes we had visitors.

Once I thought I heard
a noise outside the tent.

But the next morning
no one was there.

The day came when our vacation was over. We packed up our tent and started for home.

But we will be back
next summer!